I0673243

A Bittersweet Biography of Life with an Addicted Father

MY POOR DAD

By
Pablo
(James G D Paul)

Second edition.

All characters referenced in this book are non-fictional. In some cases names have been modified to protect the character's privacy.

ISBN: 978-0-6151-9605-3

Published on demand
By
www.Lulu.com

Processed in the United States of America

For my dear mom Lilian, my sisters
Marcia, Elizabeth and Sybil,
and my deceased brothers
Donald and Brian

Contents

A Poetic Dedication

<u>My Poor Dad</u>

A curious sip…
A casual taste…
The mortal seed is planted, innocently…

A cheerful toast…
A raucous roast…
The mortal seed germinates, vigorously…

A reckless calling…
A burning desire…
The mortal seedling blossoms, seductively…

An urgent need…
An unfortunate tradition…
The mortal vine flourishes, compulsively…

This senseless abuse…
This desperate dependency…
This cruel addiction…
The mortal fruit dominates, destructively…

This helpless alcoholic…
This lost soul…
This wasted life…
The mortal tree kills, sadly…

My poor…

Dad.

Introduction

A complex chronic psychological and nutritional disorder associated with excessive and compulsive drinking[1]. This is the definition of a phenomenon that, in 1992, cost the United States economy $246 billion; the bulk of it due to lost and impaired productivity[2]; the definition of a phenomenon that is a dispassionate destroyer of lives old and young, male and female, religious and agnostic; the definition of the phenomenon that ruined the life of my father, Festus Paul, a young, brilliant, charismatic, but hopelessly addicted alcoholic.

Alcohol abuse, as it's more commonly known, is one of the most significant social problems in modern society. In an era of unparalleled technological and scientific progress and discovery, alcohol addiction remains an enigma, a mystery unsolved, a social cancer wreaking havoc in every corner, every town, every city, every country on planet earth.

Why has society failed to find effective solutions to this problem? Are there any programs to successfully prevent and treat alcohol addiction? Do we fully understand the etiology, the root cause(s), of this disease? How can we learn from the demise of addicts and their families?

These questions, with emphasis on the latter, are the focus of this book. My goal is to narrate my experience as the son of an alcohol abuser. To take readers on a retrospective journey that begins when a six-year old boy first observes his dad in a drunken state, and ends with a father's premature death from cirrhosis of the liver, a direct consequence of alcohol abuse.

The reader will experience, first hand, the social pressures that force an impressionable teenager to take his first sip of rum; the failure of parents (my paternal grandparents) to intervene and prevent a casual habit from metastasizing into a destructive addiction; the related sexual promiscuities and infidelities; the struggle and determination of a young wife (my mother) to hold her family together in the face of rejection by her own mother; the abuse suffered by the young children of an alcohol addict; the destruction of a father's promising fire-fighting career; the gradual, deliberate and painful decay of a precious life; and the countless embarrassing, humorous, depressing and tragic experiences of a family that perseveres in the face of adversity.

The book concludes with a brief review of empirical research data on alcohol addiction to help readers better understand and appreciate its complexity and magnitude. A list of online resources is also provided to facilitate the search for answers and information on alcoholism and rehabilitative services. Please know that help is abundantly available. This is the information age. Take advantage of it...

Prologue

"Hit me!

Hit me, just one more time," my sister Liz screams, brandishing a well-sharpened machete in her right hand, inches from dad's face, "and I will chop you into a million pieces!"

Dad never hit her again.

Liz revealed this incident to me thirty years after it occurred. She spoke with passion as if reliving the moment. She spoke with pride; elated by the memory that, at the tender age of fifteen, she had found the courage to fight back, to defy her abusive step-father, my alcohol-addicted dad.

I was ten years old at the time. My younger sister, Fiona, was nine. Our mom, Irene, protected us as best she could from the turbulence of dad's drunkenness. But mom was also a victim, her radiant smile and selfless love, notwithstanding. She persevered through faith in God and a dogged determination to honor her sacred marital vows – "Until Death Do Us Part" - by any means necessary.

In mom's deeply religious mind, dad's alcoholism was merely her cross to bear and, like Jesus, she would bear it without complaint to the bitter end, regardless of the potential damaging effects on her children. She prayed daily for dad to change but he never did. He worshipped another god: RUM.

Years Later, during one of our rare conversations, I provocatively asked my dad for his best advice with regards to alcohol use. He adroitly changed the subject. But I persisted, as he fidgeted nervously, overtly discomforted by my loaded question. I relented after I saw tears welling in his eyes. My inquisition had struck too close to home.

Liz was my mother's biological daughter from an alleged sexual assault by a male acquaintance in 1954. Mom was a young, attractive, nursing student back then. Her lustrous jet black hair framed a pretty face accentuated by long eye-lashes, high regal cheekbones and full Nubian lips. Her skin was naturally stained a delicate smooth caramel courtesy of her mixed Amerindian and African heritage. Her effervescent smile lit up the room. Her personality was magnetic. Liz's biological father was the male acquaintance that allegedly couldn't control his physical lust for Irene, so he raped her…. according to Liz's version of how she was conceived.

My maternal grandmother, Lilian, the iron-willed and opinionated matriarch of the London family, was furious when she learned of mom's untimely pregnancy. Irene was the youngest of her three daughters and she was off to such a fine start professionally in a respectable career as a registered nurse, a source of inspiration to the proud family. And now this!

Mom persevered through nine months of scathing verbal abuse and name-calling of the worst kind. She had disgraced the entire family and she wouldn't hear the end of it.

Liz was born in February, 1955. She was grandma Lilian's first grandchild and became the "apple of her eye." Moreover, among the five children of James and Lilian London, Irene would be the only one to bear children of her own. How ironic!

Mom and Liz lived at grandma's house in Islington, a sleepy village located south of New Amsterdam, on the eastern coast of the Berbice River. An eclectic mix of public servants, teachers, fishermen, farmers and businessmen lived in modest homes on both sides of Islington road, a dirt-compacted extension of Main Street, New Amsterdam's primary throughway. On a typical day, an intermittent stream of pedestrians, taxi-cabs, donkey and horse-drawn carts, buses, tractors and even herds of cattle navigated back and forth over this dusty trail. A group of shirtless boys waited impatiently, metal buckets in hand, at one of the few sources of running water located in front of Grandma Lilian's home. Islington's western coastline featured a mile-long wall of reinforced concrete that protected the low-lying village from severe floods by the billowing tides of the Berbice River.

Aunt Maggie and Grandma Lilian pampered and spoiled Liz while mom continued her nursing studies. It was an unstable yet workable compromise; but not for long.

Irene re-ignited her mother's wrath when she brought home a tall, dark-skinned gentleman to ask for her hand in marriage. It was customary in those days for a male suitor to seek permission from the parents of his prospective bride.

"First you disgrace the family name by having a baby out of wedlock," grandma yelled. *"Now you want to marry this adulterer[1], this worthless black fella!"* Grandma was furious. *"Over my dead body!"*

Mom eloped and married dad anyway, leaving Liz with grandma Lilian and aunt Maggie. I was born in 1960 and my younger sister, Fiona, entered this world in 1962. This is our story.

---

[1] Adulterer: reference to dad's three children (Donald, Brian and Sybil) from a previous relationship

The Early Years

1965

I load a pebble into the leather tongue of my sling shot, firmly grasp the base of its Y-shaped frame with my raised right hand, pull the loaded tongue back with my left thumb and forefinger, and let go. The recoil of the stretched rubber catapults the pebble into the skull of a young firefighter riding his bicycle on the narrow dirt road of the Savannah Park housing complex. The young firefighter is my godfather, David. He loses control of the bike and falls onto the dirt road, bleeding profusely.

In my earliest childhood memory, I was four years old and Fiona was three. It was a lazy Sunday afternoon. We lived in a rented, two-bedroom home in Savannah Park; a residential area of single family, two-story homes in New Amsterdam. The lower level was built with cement blocks painted light blue and housed the combination living/dining room and a small kitchen. A wooden lacquered staircase ascended from the linoleum-covered ground floor to the second floor where two bedrooms and a full bathroom were located.

Dad, a firefighter, was away at work, and mom had the day off from New Amsterdam hospital where she was employed as a registered nurse, having successfully completed her nursing program. She was either preoccupied in the kitchen or taking a nap in her bedroom upstairs. Fiona and I played with our toys in the living room on the first floor.

On a whim, we decided to go to grandma's house for our favorite snacks of roly poly[2], pine drink and maybe a snow-cone of crushed ice covered in red syrup and a layer of sweetened condensed milk. We got dressed as mom cooked or slept. Since the front and back doors were both locked, I opened the lower front window on the first floor, using the dining room chair as a prop. At three feet and a few inches, I was taller and a little stronger than Fiona so I hoisted her to the ledge of the open window. She pulled

---

[2] Guyanese pastry made of a tasty grounded coconut core sweetened and dyed red, wrapped in loaves of wheat dough, baked, glazed then sliced and ready to serve.

her lean frame through and jumped to the grassy front yard a few feet below. I quickly followed her through the open window and we skipped, hand-in-hand, Fiona and I, to grandma's house. Or so we thought.

Grandma Lilian's home was actually some ten miles away. But what's a few miles to two hungry toddlers? We were more concerned with getting our favorite snacks.

After walking for some five to ten minutes, we saw "grandma's house" with its unmistakable, long, wooden platform bridge. The front door was wide open. We raced inside, scampered into a bedroom, and jumped onto the bed shouting excitedly, *"Grandma, grandma!"*

The elderly home-owner was busy washing dishes when she heard what sounded like children's voices inside the house. She dried her hands hastily on her apron and hurried to investigate. Her eyes widened in amazement at two of the cutest little children, a boy and a girl, romping playfully on her bed. They even called her "grandma." But she had no children and lived alone. Maybe this was a blessing from God, she thought. Maybe this was the answer

to her prayers.

"I ought to raise these two adorable toddlers as my own," she

pondered for a fleeting moment before dismissing the temptation.

She then opened her living room window and beckoned to a young

man living in a bungalow next door, to come over. He was a

gentleman in his mid-thirties who was recently engaged to a young

woman from Islington village. Coincidentally, the young woman,

his fiancée, was our aunt Olive, mom's sister. Clarence recognized

us instantly.

"Those are my sister-in-law Irene's kids," he exclaimed, *"I*

know them."

He took us home to our very grateful mother. She had been on

the verge of hysteria after being unable to locate her two precious

children. She had called out our names, *"Greg, Fiona, where are*

you?"... Silence. *"Greg and Fiona!"*... More silence. Her anxiety-

level had risen with each unanswered call. She was about to run

next-door for help when Clarence knocked on the door. Two

familiar faces smiled at her. Her munchkins were safe. *"Praise the Lord! Praise the Lord!"* she exclaimed. The roly-poly-pine-drink adventure was over.

Those early years were the best. Dad, robust and very sober, kept a vegetable garden in the backyard which was enclosed by a fence of thick, meshed wire anchored by six-foot high wooden posts to protect against hungry roaming bovines. Sweat trickled down his back as he worked the land; cutting, shoveling, planting, mulching and watering long dirt beds of bora, okra, callaloo and tomatoes.

"Here son. Come take a look at this earthworm," Dad called, dangling a writhing reddish muddy creature in his hand. *"This is what fishermen use as bait to catch fish."*

Dad had honed his skills as a farmer from long hours of back-breaking work with his father on the family farm in Light Town, a small village on the eastern coast of the Berbice River, south of Islington. A wrinkled, water-stained photograph from those early days displayed a tall, well-built, ebony-toned, young man flexing his muscles as he posed for the camera like a professional body-builder.

Mom, a tireless busy-body, worked a full day at the hospital then hurried home to clean, cook, iron, wash, and complete countless other household chores in between. She was quite an amazing woman. She was always buzzing like a bumble bee, doing something or the other. She was the first to rise in the morning and the last to go to bed at night. Mom escorted Fiona and me each day to our kindergarten classes at Ms. Carrington's house next door, before taking off for work on her black and silver Raleigh ladies' bicycle. She painted a pretty sight - her white nurse's cap perched like a crown on her head, tapered white uniform with blue stripes hugged her shapely body; her matching stockings and leather shoes pedaled white circles as she biked approximately two miles to work.

My godfather, David, was also a firefighter. He was like a big brother to me. He taught me how to make a sling shot, using the forked limb of a tree and rubber from dad's old bicycle tires.

Ironically, I shot him in the head with the very sling shot he had made for me. He bled quite a bit, but wasn't seriously hurt. I suspected that I must have gotten a beating from dad for that incident. I can't quite remember though.

Fiona and I did everything together. We were like inseparable twins. In fact, some of our friends thought we were twins. As innocent as our early childhood appeared, there were some dark moments. Some have faded with time, but one memory in particular haunts me to this day. Fiona and I were probably five and six years old respectively; perhaps even younger.

It was not unusual for us to go to our neighbors' homes by ourselves. In those days, all of the parents knew and looked out for each other. It was, therefore, not uncommon for children to be verbally scolded, and even spanked by a neighbor when they stepped out of line. Hence, parents never dreamt that anything untoward could ever happen to their children in the home of a neighbor. Everyone looked out for each other, remember.

In the fuzzy web of my childhood memories, an ugly incident lingers and haunts. It is a memory that involved my sister, Fiona. I didn't actually see anything occur, but I distinctly recall feeling uncomfortable when one of the Smart boys took her into a bedroom in their home and closed the door leaving me outside. She was only five years old. He was much older.

I recently discussed this haunting memory with Fiona and was much relieved when she told me that she had absolutely no recollection of any such incident.

Reflections

I have no memory of ever seeing dad drunk or even consuming alcohol during the first five years of my life. I know now that he had his first taste of alcohol in his early teens. He told me, later in life, that he drank with increasing frequency as a youth, especially on the weekends. It was a rite of passage. It meant he was grown-up. It meant he was a real man. It meant he could brag to his buddies about his notoriety as a consumer of the hard stuff.

Furthermore, it was not uncommon for older men to threaten or inflict bodily harm on young, Guyanese men if they refused to drink alcohol. Dad and his friends were threatened. Dad and his friends started drinking. Dad and many of his friends became alcoholics.

I first observed my dad in a drunken state at age six or seven.

THE EARLY YEARS

1967

"Help, help, I'm on fire!" Liz yells. Flames leap from her night gown. She runs down the wooden stairs. She jumps onto the muddy road screaming, "My legs are burning! Help me please somebody, help me!"

———————————————

Liz had recently come to live with us after we moved to a two-family house in Stanleytown, a suburb of New Amsterdam. The town was designed in a rectangular, grid-like pattern. Narrow parallel roads ran perpendicular to three wider primary streets: Water Street on the west, Main Street in the center, and Republic Road on the eastern border of the grid. Each road had a unique number. Ours was Forty Four.

The home was painted green with white trim framing the windows and doors. It was rented from a family who had relocated out-of-town. It contained three bedrooms on the second level where we lived. The lower level, a two-bedroom apartment, was leased to another family. The backyard was unfenced and a sea of leafy eddo[3] plants surrounded the cemented septic tank. Two giant trees – one, jamoon[4] and the other, bread fruit – ascended to the heavens from the corners of the yard.

Mom gave Liz, then twelve, her own bedroom. Fiona and I shared a queen-sized bed in the second bedroom. Mom and dad occupied the third.

Liz was very mature for a twelve-year old. She already knew how to cook and clean and do all of the other household chores just like mom. She was definitely a better cook. Mother's cooking was....well, let's just say, Liz's meals were tastier.

I recall that Liz was quite fond of her little brother. She tickled, rubbed my nappy head and pinched my chubby cheeks. She often braided Fiona's hair but didn't play much with her. In fact, Liz frequently spanked her with artificial flowers from mom's glass

---

[3] A tropical ground vegetable with green stalks and large heart-shaped, succulent green leaves.
[4] A wild tropical grape-sized fruit, purple-coated when ripe with a sweet fleshy seeded core; often preserved to make jamoon wine by locals.

vase on the living room table. Fiona was a feisty little girl while I was more of a mellow, easy-going kid. In retrospect, there may have been a bit of sibling rivalry, if not jealousy, behind Liz's penchant for spanking Fiona.

Our new home was more spacious than the previous one in Savannah Park. Mom and dad had settled into their respective careers and the time was right to integrate Liz into our lives. She was, after all, my mother's first born and deserved an opportunity to live with us. But I imagine that convenience was also an important factor in this decision. Liz, five years my senior, could take care of Fiona and me while mom and dad were away at work. In other words, she could be our mom-by-proxy.

Unfortunately, Liz and her step-father never developed a good relationship. I was too young to notice at the time, but Liz later told me that dad treated her more like the help than a step-daughter who needed emotional support and guidance. From Liz's perspective, mom wasn't much different either. Consequently, Liz developed feelings of insecurity and bitterness from an early age that affect her to this day.

Early one morning as Liz prepared breakfast on the gas-burning stove, something went terribly wrong. Fiona and I were still asleep when her strident screams pierced the morning air. We jumped out of bed as Liz ran down the stairs, screaming. We looked through the window. Liz was on fire, screaming louder, hands flailing wildly in the air. She ran to the neighbors for help. Fortunately, they were able to extinguish the fire but the damage had been done. Liz was taken to the hospital where she was treated for second degree burns to her legs and thighs. Welcome to the family big sis.

Growing up in an era without television or video-games, my friends and I created a variety of outdoor games and activities. One of our favorite pastimes was a game of marbles. We used shredded awara[5] seeds as marbles, dug four fist-sized holes in the dirt with our heels and took turns rolling our marbles into them. The holes

---

[5] A genus of nut-producing palm (Astrocaryum) indigenous to northern Southern America

were spaced five to six feet apart. The first player to roll his marble into all four holes was the winner. If a player missed a hole, the next player could knock his marble out of the way. That made the game more challenging. It was a primitive form of golf ...without the clubs.

"Here comes your dad," yelled Lindon, *"let's go."* Dad had warned us repeatedly not to play marbles in the yard. But we played anyway. Of course, any sign of him approaching, triggered a mad scramble. Little frantic hands gathered the marbles; little frantic feet scampered to the sanctuary of their respective homes, leaving yours truly to face the wrath of an irate father.

As a firefighter, dad worked both the day and night shifts. In my mind's eye, I pictured him going to work at the crack of dawn impeccably dressed in his navy blue uniform with red lapels. His black leather boots were always well-polished and waxed. His pants were starched and pressed with razor-sharp seams up the front and back. Shiny silver buttons ran down the front of his long-sleeved shirt. His black hat was pulled snugly over his head, the brim almost covering his eyes. He, like mom, rode his bicycle to work each day.

After a long day's work, especially those interrupted by fire emergencies, dad met with his drinking buddies at one of several rum shops on Main Street to unwind with raucous banter and laughter that grew louder over each emptied glass of El Dorado rum. It was a daily ritual for many Guyanese men. They worked all day, drank all night, blazed a weaving drunken trail home, to harass and embarrass their respective families. Wives and children were targets of verbal and physical abuse when the intoxicated heads of household arrived home. Fortunately, dinner and sleep provided some respite before the same decadent behaviors were replicated the following day.

In dad's case, he rode home drunk. If riding while drunk was a traffic violation, my poor dad was a repeat offender, many times over. He rode a dangerous slalom from the rum shop to our house. Taxi drivers honked their horns angrily, stopping or swerving their vehicles desperately to avoid hitting the inebriated firefighter. I recall, with some amusement, that his final turn into our driveway was often misjudged and he would crash, head over heels, into the wire fence lining our front yard, his fall cushioned by copious vines of dense green ivy covering the fence. The image of dad's drunken adventures on his bike is a scalding memory etched permanently in my mind.

Fiona and I observed dad's decadent behavior in detached silence. But our friends and neighbors, on occasion, laughed and teased, *"There goes drunken Festus again, ha, ha, ha, ha...!"* At first, the ridicule was quite excruciating but over time, we became more thick-skinned and shrugged off these taunts or ignored them completely.

I am so relieved I was not given my dad's name, Festus, as planned. It was so old-fashioned and would have made me the laughing stock of the entire neighborhood. *Festus! Yeeeeech!* Moreover, I was definitely not proud of him. I didn't respect him either. I did, however, respect and fear his belt; the one made of thick rawhide and a big brass buckle. Those lashes stung for several days. So I tried to avoid them as best as I could.

Dad was incensed one day after I had extracted his rubber tire from his bike without his permission. My friends and I dissected the tire into long narrow strips for our sling shots. We planned to shoot at flocks of Blue Sakis and Kiskadees[6] perched on the limbs of jamoon and breadfruit trees in our back yards. That afternoon, upon discovering his bicycle vandalized, dad waited patiently, leather belt in hand, for me to return from my avian hunt.

He ran towards me, *"Come here boy! I am going to teach you a lesson you'll never forget."* He reached out to grab me but I gave him a double move and ran away. I didn't look back. I ran bare-footed down the pebble-strewn path of Forty Fourth Street, turned right onto Water Street, jumped over potholes, and raced by curious pedestrians, lean legs churning, wiry arms pumping, challenged lungs gasping for air. I finally stopped for a breather at the garbage dump, a local landfill across from the cemetery, a mile

---

[6] Tropical birds of Guyana

away from my home. Dad couldn't and didn't follow me. I was too

swift. He was out-of-shape anyway.

Chest heaving from exhaustion, I sat on a discarded tire for

what seemed like an eternity. I sat alone, sulking, defiant, avoiding

eye-contact with passersby but secretly hoping that someone would

at least stop to ask why an eight-year old boy was hanging out in a

malodorous refuse dump at six o'clock in the afternoon. No one

did; so I gazed at the crimson sun's gradual descent below the tree-

lined western skyline of the Berbice River. A veil of darkness soon

enveloped the town.

An hour later, I rose from my make-shift rubber bench,

knowing that my dad would have by that time, left home for the

evening shift at the firehouse. Under the cover of night, I returned

home. Mom, Liz and Fiona were thrilled to see me. The following

day, dad was too drunk to remember my transgression.

* * *

There were some joyous times though. Like the train-rides from

Rosignol to Georgetown to visit relatives and family friends. Mom always bought new gear for us to wear on those excursions. In the Guyanese vernacular we wore our "Sunday's best".

My hair was freshly cut, exposing an unusually large head *(hence, my nickname – "Big Head Pablo, De Man Dat De Bakoo Box"[7])*. A navy blue bow-tie hugged the collar of my lily white, short-sleeved, cotton shirt neatly tucked into my khaki short pants, exposing my well-greased, scrawny, black legs in knee-high, blue socks and black, glistening bulldogs[8].

Fiona's neatly-braided ponytails protruded from her tiny head like a pair of lustrous black horns, each circled by a red ribbon bow. A white, plastic barrette secured a fashionable bang gracing the top of her precious heart-shaped face; *(her nick name was Ka Ka Way Way – inspiration unknown)*. A pretty, pink dress trimmed in white lace closely circled her waist, and fell with a wide flourish just below her knees. Her matching pink socks were neatly folded above her ankles. Little white shoes with straps and silver buckles added the final touch. The little princess smiled cheerfully as we

---

[7] Guyanese creolese (slang) meaning: "…the man who was slapped in the head by an evil spirit."
[8] Shoes with a huge rounded tip

walked, hand-in-hand, behind mom and dad to the corner of Forty-Fourth and Main. Dad hailed a cab to take us to New Amsterdam's harbor for the ride by ferry across the Berbice River.[9]

Liz *(a.k.a. Big Bertha -she was blessed with a few extra but shapely pounds)* never made these trips with us. For reasons unknown, she was left behind, like an unwanted step-child, at Grandma Lilian's home in Islington village.

The ferry- Torani[10] - blared a final boarding call as late-arriving passengers rushed to get on board. We climbed the winding wooden stairs to the upper level where we cautiously stepped over the lowered door into the passenger seating area. A young crewman clad in blue denims and a white sailor's cap, pulled the heavy steel doors shut. Another able-bodied seaman removed the hefty ropes looped around anchor posts on the wooden wharf, hurled them onto the lower deck, and hopped on board. With two terminal toots, S.S. Torani departed for Rosignol.

---

[9] Creolese term meaning "wharf or docking station for boats."
[10] Name of passenger boat

We sat on wooden benches on the deck as the ferry traversed the muddy, cresting waves of the Berbice River on a breezy cruise from New Amsterdam to Rosignol. The river ran from a narrow southern source deep in the green Amazonian forests of Berbice, and descended through a yawning northern channel into the colossal swell of the Atlantic Ocean. Rosignol's wharf appeared much smaller in the distance as we sailed across the mile-wide river. We gazed inquisitively at dark-skinned Indo-Guyanese fishermen, half-naked in their canoes, hustling with netting gear, pulling a fresh catch on board. They waved to us as we sailed by. We waved back at them. A flock of grayish-white sea gulls skimmed to the river's surface, plumed wings flapping furiously in the wind as they pursued a piscine meal. After thirty minutes or so, we arrived at Rosignol, disembarked and walked to the train station.

Dad purchased our tickets and we hopped on board the train. Fiona and I sat at window seats in a private cabin opposite each other. We pressed our faces against the cold glass window and stared at the commotion outside. Local vendors rushed to the side of the train. Women and girls of Indian and African descent carried bamboo baskets filled with assorted foods and fruits for sale. They literally balanced these basket trays on their heads. I was always quite amazed that the baskets never fell as they jostled and competed with each other to earn a quick dollar before the train pulled off.

"Get yo fudge and pine tart ova hey," one yelled. *"Fry fish and bread, Polourie and mitai dis side,"* shouted another.

Soon the train departed for the big city. Fiona and I settled into our seats momentarily to munch on snacks, before resuming our curious vigil at the train's window. Several loud blasts from the train's horns signaled the start of our journey. Puffs of smoke from the locomotive's furnace leaped into the morning sky. Iron wheels rotated with crunching refrain on paired metal rails stretched on a raised bed of thick wooden slabs, broken rocks and compacted dirt. The hectic, colorful scenery of the Rosignol rail station gradually disappeared as the train's massive engines gathered momentum.

Clusters of wooden and mud-stained homes, and open pastures ran up then receded as we passed through village after village after village on our train ride to Georgetown.

"Look mom, look at those cows," Fiona pointed to a herd of Brahman cattle being herded by an Afro-Guyanese youth waving a stick in his right hand.

I marveled at the long stretches of rice fields, a sweeping sea of tall green, grassy stalks dancing in the wind, bordered by man-made dams. Farmers worked the land on their muddy tractors and red combines. Fishermen, nets held high over their shoulders, stood knee-deep in trenches, hoping to catch a few hassa and patwa[11] for lunch and dinner.

The train ride lasted a few hours with several stops along the way to pick up and unload passengers and freight from farmers and hucksters traveling to the city to peddle their merchandise in Stabroek and Bourda markets.[12]

---

[11] Scaled fish indigenous to northern South America
[12] The two primary markets in Georgetown, Guyana

Located on the north-eastern coast of Guyana, Georgetown, the Garden City, was framed by the Demerara river on the west and the Atlantic ocean/Caribbean sea to the north. The city was originally designed as a fort by the early Dutch colonialists to protect their settlements along the Demerara River. Expansive tree-lined avenues and irrigation canals formed a distinct, tourist-friendly, rectangular pattern. Several historic wooden buildings constructed in the 18th and 19th centuries enhanced the tropical, exotic ambience of the nation's capital. The most prominent structures were: St. George's Cathedral - one of the largest free-standing wooden buildings in the world; Stabroek Market – Guyana's largest market, designed and built by the Dutch, and featured a prominent red and white tower; the Parliament building and Law Courts. Other points of interest included: the extensive Sea Wall to the north that protected the low-lying city from severe floods; the Botanical Gardens with a plethora of exotic, colorful tropical flora (hence the Garden City moniker); the Wildlife Zoo, and the Durban Park race track.

While in Georgetown, we visited the Zoo or Botanical Gardens as well as the homes of relatives and family friends. Fiona and I kept busy reading children's books or teasing each other as mom and dad conversed with our hosts. The highlight of our visits to the Garden City, from my perspective, was lunch or dinner at Demico House, a very popular restaurant located next to Stabroek market. The baked chicken and ice cream desserts were finger-licking good. After a toothsome meal, we returned, tired and stuffed, to the train station for the long ride home.

Reflections

The burden of sadness is lessened, albeit temporarily, by a change of scenery, a quick get-away, a well-deserved vacation. This effectively recharges worn batteries, renews the spirit, and offers a ray of hope for those who persevere. Despite the painful memories of dad's drunken decadence, despite the embarrassing experiences, there were moments of joy, of happy times.... and for that I am very grateful.

Dad's health, however, would take a turn for the worst, taxing the limited resources of his family, challenging the faith and resolve of best ally - his loving wife.

THE EARLY YEARS

1968

"What's my name dad?" I ask. He stares at me with vacuous eyes, detached from reality. His face is swollen. His hands shake involuntarily. "De...De...Desta," he mumbles my middle name hesitantly. His speech is slurred. His memory is almost shot. He needs help walking. Mom feeds him. My once-able dad is now a helpless patient. He is stricken by a life-threatening illness caused by his alcohol abuse. Mom, the ever- faithful wife, secures the best treatment she could find for him. She takes him to see a psychiatrist in Georgetown. He is lucky to have her as his wife. Most women would have left him a long time ago.

All was relatively calm after we moved from Savannah Park to Stanleytown. Mom worked. Dad worked and drank. My sisters and I attended school. Then my poor dad got mentally ill. It was some sort of alcohol-induced psychosis.

Mom tried her best. She spent every penny she earned to feed, house, clothe, educate, and, on occasion, buy us a few treats. We were enrolled, Liz, Fiona and I, in the best private Anglican school in New Amsterdam: Scarder's Preparatory School.

The principal, Mr. Scarder was a strict, no-nonsense educator and disciplinarian. He was feared by student and teacher alike. His teaching philosophy was simple: '*…if you couldn't learn, your butt would burn!*' He motivated us with the whip of his bamboo cane. Every student either gave Mr. Scarder their undivided attention or paid a painful price. It was not uncommon for him to scurry down the center aisle, whipping his cane from side to side, across the bare hands, heads, backs and any other vulnerable body part of students in the class room. This mass flogging took place daily, especially if we failed to provide the correct answers to simple questions.

And we all got personalized attention from our exacting principal during his much-dreaded Arithmetic class. Many of us doubled-up on our underwear and pants to cushion the bite of Mr.

Scarder's bamboo cane on our backsides. It was not uncommon for him to summon us individually to the front of the class to challenge our mathematical aptitude.

"Five plus eight plus nine plus twelve equals ……..?" He asked in rapid fashion, giving me a split second to answer, his cane raised and ready to strike.

"Thirty-four," I answered, holding my breath.

"Correct," said the cane master. *"Next student."*

I exhaled in relief and returned wide-eyed to my bench as the next student/victim walked with much trepidation towards the blackboard.

We learned by rote and intimidation in those days. We recited the multiplication tables daily, sang the national anthem, pledged allegiance to the flag of Guyana, wrote essays, practiced math, attended extra classes on Saturdays, and prepared for the national Common Entrance Exams. A good score meant acceptance into the best high schools. A poor one was a ticket to technical or vocational school for a career as a tradesman or clerk. Most of us did fairly well. My grades placed me into Overwinning Government Secondary School (O.G.S.S. now Berbice High School); Fiona's got her into Berbice Educational Institute (B.E.I.) and Liz transferred to Tutorial High, a secondary school in Georgetown..

The foundation for my future academic success was reinforced by my primary school teachers, self-motivation, and the intimidating presence of Mr. Scarder. Undoubtedly, mom and dad provided the basics of shelter, food and clothing, but a child needs more. Now that I am a parent, I have a unique appreciation of the value of investing quality time with young children to help them navigate the stormy seas of education and life. Mom probably compensated for her short-comings in this area of child development by sending us to private schools.

Despite mom's best efforts to shelter us from the raging storm of dad's self-destructive behavior, the images of his demise were indelibly etched in my memory. His transition from casual to compulsive consumption of alcohol took an enormous toll on his health and the quality of our lives. Slowly, steadily his vigor and strength waned. The sanguine, able-bodied firefighter became an unkempt, hostile stranger. Parenting was the least of his concerns. Dad was infected by a potent virus named addiction; his brain was re-programmed to continuously crave the intoxicating sensation of his next drink. Alcohol was his elixir. Everything else became insignificant: his wife, his kids, his job, his health, his life....

* * *

My poor Dad sat in silence at our dining table. His weight had ballooned to over two hundred and fifty pounds. His hands hung limply by his side. His eyes held a blank forlorn stare. When he tried to speak, the words were mumbled and barely comprehensible. To my juvenile mind, the scene was surreal. On one level, I clearly knew that the man sitting at the table was my dad; on another, it was difficult to comprehend why he couldn't remember the names of his children, or speak coherently, or feed himself. Dad was a far cry from the robust young man flexing his muscles proudly in the afore-mentioned photograph. He now relied on mom to hold his hands as he shuffled his feet unsteadily around the house.

Dad was deathly ill. He was diagnosed with alcohol-induced psychosis, a secondary psychosis with predominant symptoms of hallucination caused by chronic alcoholism. He was fortunate to have a wife who was a psychiatric nurse. Mom arranged consultations and treatment by the best psychiatrists in Guyana.

Over the next few months, dad gradually recovered; he regained his memory and shed several pounds. I later learned that his weight-gain was a common side-effect of the anti-psychotic medications he had received for his illness. Still, he looked very weak and fragile. Eventually, thanks largely to therapy administered by mom, his speech and gait improved and he regained his strength. It was a close call. Alcohol-induced psychosis almost took his life. Perhaps this was his wake-up call. Perhaps he would stop drinking.

He started drinking again.

* * *

In 1969, Mom and dad bought our first home; a cozy three-bedroom, single-family home in a new cooperative housing development, Tucber Park, on the north side of town. Working class families were targeted by the developers to purchase and occupy these homes. Each of the first fifty homes were built on a rectangular lot approximately one-fifth of an acre in size. A ten-foot wide drainage and irrigation canal ran down the center of Tucber Park and emptied into Canje Creek, a black water tributary of the Berbice river that weaved through the dense forests to the east. We were among the first group of home-owners to move into the new development. It was a very proud moment for us.

Reflections:

We are each dealt different cards in the game of life, some tragic, horrible, heart-breaking; others wonderful, spectacular, amazing. We have to play the hand we are dealt or get out of the game. As children in the home of an alcohol abuser, mom, my sisters and I were all victims. Without access to resources such as

alcohol-awareness and rehabilitative programs, we did the best we
could to survive.

Could mom have done more to confront dad about his abuse of
alcohol   Sure.

Was she too naïve thinking that prayers alone would
miraculously change her reality for the better?   Yes.

Was dad worth the effort?   Absolutely.

Was his addiction so powerful that even the best alcohol
rehabilitative programs would have been a waste of time and
money? Who knows?

Did mom get any or enough support from immediate family and
friends?   No.

These questions linger to this day. These questions inspire me to
conduct research into the etiology of alcoholism; to write this
book; to extend a helping hand to the addicted whenever possible.
I could have chosen the easy way out and blame dad's dysfunction
as the reason for my lack of motivation and success. But I choose
not to repeat the mistakes of my poor dad. I choose to stay on a

positive path and win in the game of life. I choose to pursue knowledge, fulfillment and self-actualization. I choose to avoid destructive vices. I choose to prosper.

Dad made his choices too and they were about to ruin his career and his life.

THE EARLY YEARS

1969

Our very own home!

Fiona and I run up the front stairs, dash through the white front door and explore every room and fixture in the house. Mom buys a new bunk bed which meant I no longer had to share sleeping space with Fiona. Yes! We make new friends with the Clarks, Ramsays, Ferdinands, Johnsons, Hazelwoods, to name a few, all proud first-time home owners. My family is proud too. But a sinister cloud hangs over us, threatening to burst, to ruin the pride of first-time home-ownership and destroy our hope for a brighter future. It is dad's alcohol addiction. Mom tries desperately to hold the fragile cloud together, but it bursts and wreaks havoc on our psychological and financial well-being.

It was our first Christmas at the new house. Everyone was excited. Mom and Liz shopped for colorful window treatments and holiday decorations. Dad tinkered with the stove like the handyman he wasn't. Fiona and I, eight and nine respectively, played a game of hide-and-seek, running like little mice, in and out of closets, scuttling under beds and behind window blinds. Christmas, the celebration of the birth of Jesus Christ, was always a time of fun and good cheer for all children. We were no different.

Christmas meant flashing red, white and green lights through every window and, a surge of shoppers in every store. It meant fancy clothing and toys for kids and, a new make-over for homes. It meant colorful masquerade bands in the streets with Long Lady in her purple and pink polka dot dress, prancing on stilts, Po Boy in his straw hat, thumping on drums, Blackie dancing back and forth in his red float costume shaped like a bull, long wooden horns dashing playfully at children who screamed and fled with a mixture of fear and glee. And, of course, Auntie Come-See, face painted green, twirling with her tin cup, collecting money.

Christmas Eve was the big night; the most euphoric night of the year; the one night children were free. Free from the watchful, protective eyes of moms and dads. Free to act like fools and even be grown-ups for a few fleeting hours. Some puffed on cigarettes, coughing uncontrollably through a cloud of smoke; others sipped on Banks beer, grimacing; some hugged and kissed their girlfriends for the first time, ecstatic; and others simply ran like prisoners on a jail-break, shooting capped toy guns, playing cowboys and Indians, yelling at the top of their lungs. It was always a night of fun and revelry which sadly ended with the first hint of sunrise in the morning sky, when tired, aching feet would begin the long trek home , minds aglow with memories to last a lifetime.

The mouth-watering aroma of traditional Christmas treats - roast beef, baked stuffed-chicken, and pepper pot - filled the air, as I opened the front door of our new home. I smiled while savoring the delicious scent. My eyes were dazzled by the colorful radiance of new Christmas decorations and window treatments. Mom and

Liz had spent the entire evening on a dramatic home-makeover. I tasted some stuffing from the baked chicken in the oven and hurried to bed. Sleep was a priority now, breakfast would come later.

After the festive season ended we returned to our normal daily routines. But something was not right. Mom seemed pensive and distressed. Her smile had lost its luster. Dad didn't come home most nights; he was probably too drunk to navigate the simple path from the rum shop to his house. He didn't go to work either. Mom never said a word to us, but we heard and felt the anguish and disgust in her voice partially muted by the closed bedroom door, as she chastised him about his drunken, disgraceful behavior, pleading with him to stop. But he didn't.

He couldn't.

Alcohol was directing the show. He was merely a powerless actor.

It was no surprise to anyone when dad's alcohol dependence began to impair his performance as a firefighter. But while mom tried her very best to protect him from himself, his superiors at work were under no obligation to ignore his frequent tardiness and dereliction of duty. Dad was eventually placed on probation for being intoxicated on the job. His professional world slowly disintegrated into a wreck, a run-away train with a defunct braking system, rolling precipitously downhill to a finite date with disaster.

My poor dad, I am told, was very talented…. when sober; his classmates in high school remembered him as a bright and gifted student who often tutored them in various subjects; his buddies at the fire station recalled a charismatic leader with uncanny intelligence and wit, a respected firefighter designated as the most-likely to succeed, most likely to ascend to the coveted position of fire chief….when sober. But his addiction got in the way and he was ultimately left with two choices: retire or be fired.

According to mom's version of dad's professional demise, the beginning of the end occurred when dad was promoted to the position of inspector of the fire station at New Amsterdam.

Dad had been out drinking and cavorting all day with a few of his fellow firemen and drinking buddies. He was scheduled to supervise the night shift, but was so inebriated, he passed out. His buddies took him back to the firehouse. Someone called and reported a fire emergency later that night. The firefighter in charge, the recently-promoted inspector, my drunken father, never heard it. He was fast asleep in his cot. His men responded without him.

The next day, one of his drinking buddies reported the incident to the superior officers. They were livid. That was gross negligence. Festus Paul had become an embarrassment to every fire-fighter in the division, and an insult to the integrity of the proud and honorable profession of fire-fighting. This unacceptable conduct was the final straw that broke the addict's back. He had to go.

The promise, talent, and potential were never realized. Dad's dependence on alcohol destroyed his career, his family, and his life. His reputation was irrevocably tarnished by that incident and he would never be the same again. In fact, his alcohol-related tardiness and absenteeism got even worse. The end of his firefighting career was imminent.

Fortunately, mom knew some folks in high places and they came to dad's rescue. Instead of being fired, he was granted early retirement due to illness.

Reflections

As children, my sisters and I never questioned mom about issues such as: Why isn't dad working any more? Why is he always drunk? Why can't you do something about it? But these issues affected us at various levels and we suppressed those feelings. Mom was, in a strange way, an accomplice in dad's demise. She built a wall of secrecy to hide the hurt, shame and disgrace mutating from benign to malignant like cancerous cells at the core of our emotions.

We are all accountable for our actions and decisions as adults. However, children, teenagers and young adults living at home with their parents need guidance, counsel and tough love. In the absence of such direction, children often make poor choices. We were no exception.

In fact, we all made very poor decisions: from fornication and sexual promiscuity, to teenage pregnancies and even pregnancy terminations.

THE MIDDLE YEARS

1972 – 1977

Dad's alcohol addiction soon hit rock bottom. Betrayed and abandoned by his firefighting buddies, he suddenly looks twenty years older. He has become the prototypical town-drunk. He rarely showers, smells like stale alcohol, sleeps on sidewalks and in trenches, and is run over by a sugarcane truck. He even falls off the deck of our home. He consumes anything with a trace of alcohol in it: 'bush rum[13]*, mentholated spirit, kerosene, until he is finally arrested and sent to jail.*

⋯⋯⋯⋯⋯⋯⋯⋯⋯⋯⋯⋯

Fiona and I were both very active in sports as teenagers. Naturally gifted with the speed of a gazelle, Fiona excelled as a sprinter in high school and often represented the county of Berbice at the annual national inter-county athletic championships. My

---

[13] Home-made rum like moonshine

buddies and I played cricket, football (soccer), ran, jumped, swam, hunted, and wrestled. If a game was played in our neighborhood, we participated. This experience made me stronger both physically and mentally. Then there was high school.

I survived the first two and a half years of high school by divine grace. I participated in every extra-curricular activity offered at Overwinning Government Secondary School (OGSS). Recess and lunch breaks were the highlight of my day. Academics were another matter. I managed to score just enough on my tests to advance through the first three grades or forms, to use the British vernacular. Then it happened; the moment in my life when my nonchalance vis-à-vis academia changed forever. I called it my Eureka moment.

It was the end of the first term of my third year in high school and report cards had just been handed out to the entire class. My good buddy, Willy, and I were looking at each other's grade report when he realized that, by a few decimal points, he had finally gotten a better grade than I did.

"*Ha, ha, ha.*," Willy was overjoyed. "*I beat you Greg. I finally beat you. I got a better grade than you… dummy. Ha, ha!*"

Willy, a perennial underachiever, was so elated by this remarkable accomplishment that he teased me relentlessly for the remainder of the week. The Christmas break couldn't come fast enough.

I was furious at Willy's taunting, but he was a big kid, so physical retaliation was out of the question. I decided to use my wits instead and made a personal vow that Willy would never, ever beat me again. He didn't. In fact, my erudite buddy flunked out in the fourth form (11th grade) and was held back while yours truly advanced to the fifth form. I had the last laugh after all.

* * *

My poor dad, by this time, was the designated drunk of the town. "*There goes drunken Festus again,*" was a common refrain among my friends and neighbors. Every derogatory comment about my dad's alcohol addiction felt like a dagger through my soul. Though each remark left a profound emotional scar, I learned to hide those scars from the world.

During my teenage years, my closest friends tried their best to ease the embarrassment I felt as a result of my dad's problems. They never laughed, at least not in my presence, If we encountered my father in a drunken stupor, tripping over his tangled feet into a gutter, too inebriated to even recognize his own son. Instead they helped me drag him out of the muddy ditch and together, we took him home safely. I am sure they all had a funny story to relate to their families later. But this was no laughing matter to me. This was my life in raw and living color.

Then there is the day dad fell off a truck and was accidentally run over yet survived to tell one of his tall tales about his invincibility. According to dad, he had hitched a ride on a truck that transported employees of the sugar cane factory to their homes after a long day of back-breaking labor in the cane fields. As the truck approached the entrance to our housing development, dad attempted to jump off while the vehicle was moving, as most of the younger and more fleet-footed workers did. Neither young nor fleet-footed, my poor dad fell onto the road and the rear wheel of the truck ran over his feet. However, he quickly rose, assured the concerned driver that he was okay and sauntered home.

I witnessed dad's second accident a few months later. Slightly inebriated, he sat on the railing at the top of the front stairs to our home, basking in the cool evening breeze. The front door was wide open. As I passed by the door, he suddenly lost his balance and fell backwards over the rail to the cemented yard, some fifteen feet below. I ran down the stairs to make sure he was okay. Like a cat with multiple lives, my dad bounced to his feet. He told me that he had utilized his instinct and training as a fireman to break his fall, thus avoiding any injury. My poor dad was either lucky, as strong as an ox, or both.

* * *

The circumstances related to dad's brief incarceration are fuzzy at best. Mom was very secretive about such matters. But I later learned that he had been caught distilling and /or consuming bush rum (the Guyanese equivalent of moonshine), which was illegal. He had been warned several times by the authorities but, addicted as he was, he continued his illicit activities. And so our dad became a jailbird.

This was most embarrassing to me and I recall being very ashamed about it. Jail, in the Guyanese culture, was a place decent people avoided. It was reserved for the most decadent elements of society like murderers, thieves and rapists. My poor dad was now a part of that element.

* * *

As I grew older, I gravitated towards a number of intriguing hobbies. An older friend played in the local steel-band, Winkleaires, and invited me one afternoon after school to watch him play the first pan[14]. He taught me how to play the instrument over the next few weeks and soon I was proficient enough to join the band. At ten, I was one of the youngest band members. We practiced daily under the home of the band leader, Don. There

---

[14] A musical instrument cut from a metal drum in which musical notes are carved with a hammer, chisel and tuner. First pan is the lead (tenor) instrument made from a single drum.

were a total of fifteen to twenty members and we played at clubs,

private parties, fairs and concerts. Many of these events were local

but a few were out-of-town.

My fondest memory as a steel pan player was the 1970 Guyana

Music Festival at the National Park in Georgetown. Winkleaires

was selected to represent the county of Berbice in the steel pan

competition. Don chose me to compete in the solo, first pan event.

I used every spare minute I could squeeze from the day to practice

my rendition which was a relatively complex, classical piece. My

confidence grew with the support and encouragement of the entire

band, but there was one little catch. I was less than five feet tall.

The solo pan's stand was designed for players who were at least

five feet tall.

The photograph on the front page of the Guyana Graphic[15] the

following day featured the youngest steel pan player at the festival

standing on a short stack of books. In his hands were two wooden

pan sticks with rubber tips held high above his head, poised to

---

[15] National newspaper of Guyana in 1970.

strike the chiseled keys of the glistening first pan. You guessed it. That famous young boy was yours truly. I was so proud of that moment that I showed the newspaper to all of my neighborhood friends.

"That's me. That's me." I shouted, pointing at the paper in my hand, *"My photograph is on the front page of Graphic."*

Neither mom nor dad attended the Festival. Thus, they missed the once-in-a-lifetime experience of witnessing their proud, young son in his finest hour as a pan-man.

* * *

In 1972, after spending a few years attending Tutorial high school in Georgetown, my older sister, Liz, returned to live with us in Tucber Park. She came with some startling news. She was pregnant. Liz was only seventeen years old.

I'm sure mom was very disappointed but I was eleven at the time and Liz was probably in her third trimester when I first noticed that her stomach was protruding a little more than usual.

Apparently, she had gotten involved romantically with a young man in Georgetown. He eventually came to visit her in New Amsterdam and seemed like an honorable and responsible fellow. In fact, he proposed to Liz a few years later and they became husband and wife with a young toddler named Gwendolyn.

Gwendolyn was born on Election Day 1973 in our home. Early that morning Liz told mom she was experiencing stomach cramps. Mom sent Fiona to call our neighbor, Nurse Ramsay, a mid-wife at New Amsterdam hospital. Together, the two nurses delivered a healthy baby girl. I became a proud uncle for the first time.

Liz , meanwhile, launched her career as a trader to make ends meet and to support her daughter. She leased a booth in the local market and started sewing and selling a line of baby's and children's clothing along with other popular merchandise such as ladies sandals, shoes and cosmetic jewelry. She was a natural sales person with a sound business mind. Her career flourished and she became one of the more successful traders in New Amsterdam.

My first real job was actually as a sales assistant for Liz in her booth on Saturdays. I do not recall my exact salary but I don't remember complaining about it either. So it must have been good enough to meet the needs of a teenager.

My favorite pastime was football (soccer). My best buddy, Adrian, and I were the youngest players at thirteen and eleven respectively, on the Falcons F.C. under-16 football team. I had grown to a full five feet, not including the two-inch Afro on my head. Adrian was a few inches taller. Soccer lore has it that we were both gifted players with the skills, moves and flair to excel at the more senior and national levels as we got older.

As predicted, Adrian was selected to Guyana's national Under-19 football squad in 1977. My honor came the following year when I was chosen as a starting mid-field player for the Inter-Guiana Soccer Tournament in neighboring, Surinam. Again, neither mom nor dad ever saw me play the game of soccer. Fiona was my biggest fan and often attended many of my games at both the club and national levels.

* * *

I relocated to Guyana's capital city of Georgetown in 1977 to attend Saint Roses High School and play for Santos Football Club, one of the premier teams in the nation. The head coach, Sarjo France, recruited me to play for the Under 19 and senior squads.

A few years earlier, I took a brief hiatus from football to concentrate on my studies for the General Certificate of Education (GCE) high school exams. I soon developed a blue-collar approach to my studies; the more I read and practiced math and essay writing, the better I became. My grades improved significantly and I felt confident enough to take on six subjects in the 1976 High School exams: Geography, English, English Literature, Modern Mathematics, History and General Science.

My mother was very supportive of my efforts to succeed academically. I had a rigid routine after school each day: ride home on the bus, do my chores, finish my homework, eat an early dinner, sleep for four to five hours, and rise around 2:00 am in the morning to study the designated subject(s) on the study schedule posted on the wall of my bedroom. Mom made sure I slept undisturbed and, being an early riser herself, she always made me a warm cup of 'balgo', a mixture of hot milk, raw eggs, sugar and vanilla extract. She told me this was good food for the brain.

Fiona and I attended the local Anglican Church most Sundays where we worshipped with many of our friends and neighbors. Father Goodrich, a tall bespectacled Englishman, was the head pastor there and he knew most of us on a first name basis. He also remembered, without fail, the names of anyone who missed service on any given Sunday. Dressed in his trademark white robe, Father Goodrich made weekly rides on his old motor-cycle around the streets of our housing scheme reprimanding and reminding us to attend church. This spiritual grounding helped me develop a sound value system based on a sense of right and wrong; it also made be fully appreciate the power of prayer.

* * *

My family was touched by tragedy in the mid to late seventies when dad's oldest son, Donald, died in a drowning accident, and a few years later, dad's mom passed away in Georgetown. Donald was a very bright, charismatic and gregarious young man. He and dad's other children, Sybil and Brian, lived with their mom in Georgetown. However, each of them spent time with us in Berbice on separate occasions.

Donald was the first to visit and we bonded instantly. He was everything I had dreamed of in a big brother: cool, supportive, knowledgeable, strong, funny and experienced with the ladies.

Sybil caused quite a stir in our neighborhood when she arrived for a brief vacation. Blessed with the beauty and curves of Aphrodite, she attracted the attention of amorous suitors like honey to a swarm of bees.

Brian came a few years later. By that time he had embraced the Rastafarian culture and weed-smoking habits. Every bit of promise he possessed literally went up in smoke as his life spiraled out of control ending with his tragic death at the hands of crazed neighbor in his hometown several years later.

Donald's accident hit us the hardest. He was on the verge of completing his one-year stint of National Service at Kimbia and commencing his studies at Tuskegee University in Alabama, when the cruel hands of fate ended his life. Donald was only twenty four years old.

My poor dad had the unenviable task of identifying the body of his first born son in the morgue at Georgetown hospital. It had taken rescuers several days to recover Donald's body from the lake into which he had made his ultimate dive. Dad's voice broke as he described the condition of his son's corpse.

"A large chunk of your brother's face was missing, Gregory. He was barely recognizable."

* * *

Dad continued his love affair with El Dorado, bush rum, and other alcohol-based inebriants. He was merely a figure-head in our home; a disheveled, unkempt sad caricature spiraling down destiny's slippery slope with neither the will nor means to stop. Sister Paul, my enterprising, church-going, hymn-singing, always-smiling mother did double duty as mom and dad. We managed to survive on her meager income of one hundred and twenty dollars monthly. Somehow, she provided the food, toys, clothing, and allowance my sisters and I needed. We never felt deprived, except towards the end of the month when her salary ran out. On those days, we learned to enjoy black tea (i.e. without milk) and meatless dinners. A variety of fruits - mango, guava, sugar cane and coconut – flourished on trees in our backyard and took the edge off our hunger during the lean days. Mom also prepared a vegetable garden of calaloo, bora, cabbage and wiri wiri peppers that helped as well.

* * *

The fee for the G.C.E. examination was one hundred and twenty dollars, exactly one month's salary for mom. The deadline was just a few weeks away. If mom weren't able to pay this bill, my intensive preparation would have been for naught.

Miraculously, she raised the necessary funds and I registered for the examination. I resolved to make everyone - mom, my sisters, my friends; my neighbors.....even my poor dad - proud of Big Head Pablo.

Reflections

Mothers, daughters and sons living in homes with alcohol-addicted husbands and fathers, find ways to cope that are truly amazing. Looking back on my life, I salute my mother, her short-comings notwithstanding, for persevering, for finding a way, for ensuring that my sisters and I got a decent education, or at least the opportunity to secure one. She recently revealed to me that she always tried to isolate us as much as possible from dad's drunkenness. She thought that a larger home would minimize our interaction with our alcoholic father. In reality, it did not but, at least, she tried.

Thanks mom.

At some point, my sisters and I realized that in spite of the troubling circumstances of our family life, there were other children in our community being raised under conditions that were significantly worse. Some of our closest friends namely Jeff Roberts and Colin Ross, lived with single moms and several siblings, yet found a way to survive.

My sisters and I developed strong personalities and this, coupled with our emotional baggage, would put us at odds with each other. As mom's middle child, I became the mediator, the finder of common ground as the seeds of a profound rift within our family began to sprout.

THE FINAL YEARS

1978 - 1981

I fidget in the back seat of my school bus which is loaded with classmates from Saint Roses High. We are returning to Georgetown from a field trip to New Amsterdam. I had agreed, with much reservation, for the class to make a surprise visit to my home in Tucber Park. I pray and hope that my father isn't home. That he is out somewhere, anywhere, getting his drink on.

Career counseling was rare if not absent during my high school years. Serendipity was my guidance counselor. At first, I wanted to be a geologist, then an anthropologist, then an engineer, then a math teacher, before finally settling on veterinary medicine. Ultimately, I became a Pharmaceutical Sales Representative, writer and poet. Go figure!

At the tender age of fifteen, I had already demonstrated the discipline and commitment to academics by excelling on the national GCE exams. In retrospect though, I wish I had a mentor, someone to help me connect my interests and talents to a viable and rewarding career. I ended up drifting, changing career choices, majors, jobs; being good at several endeavors, but never rising to a level of expertise in any, never fully maximizing my intellectual potential.

On the positive side, I learned to be independent at an early age; to make my own choices; to be my own man, though I was still a teenager. With my mom busy working, doing double parental duty, and sheltering us from dad's addiction, I really had no choice but to find my own way.

After my first year in the advanced level class or sixth form at New Amsterdam Multilateral High School, I gave up on English Literature, Geography and a future as a geologist, to join the Hinterland Development Program (HDP) at Saint Roses High School. It was marketed as a dynamic combination of academic theory and practical, hands-on training. The two-year curriculum was supposed to be equivalent to the GCE sixth-form standard. The noted advantage was that students who completed HDP would be equipped with practical and technical skills better-suited to the developing agriculture-based Guyanese economy.

The HDP advertisement in the classified section of the Guyana Graphic caught my eye. The curriculum was much more appealing than another year interpreting the likes of Shakespeare, Chaucer and Sir Edgar Allan Poe. So, on my own, I applied. My letter of acceptance arrived a few weeks later. I informed my mother and a few weeks later, I packed a large suitcase with a few personal effects and took off for Georgetown to commence my studies at Saint Rose's High School.

This was my first time away from my family for any extended period. It was the equivalent of going away to college. I was nervous and excited; concerned about adjusting to life in the big city but elated to get away from dad's drunken antics.

* * *

I was probably fourteen years old when the local telecommunications company, GTC, installed our first telephone, a shiny black device with a rotary dial. Prior to this, our main modes of communication were word-of-mouth, mail, radio and telegraph. Only a privileged few experienced the luxury of television in their homes. My family was definitely not among them.

Our old reliable green transistor radio connected us with the rest of the country and the world; we listened to the news, to popular music, to Muhammad Ali fights, to cricket and football matches, to soap operas like "Dr Paul", and to the daily death announcements at nine p.m.

I distinctly remember a group of my closest friends hunched over the radio listening intently to "The Rumble in the Jungle", yelling and arguing as Ali used the rope-a-dope to befuddle, frustrate and eventually knock out George Foreman in the eight round. Dad occasionally made a sober appearance to chat with my friends as we listened to various sporting events. He and mom both possessed the gift of gab and could easily carry a conversation for hours without breaking a sweat. I often had to remind them that my friends were my guests not theirs.

* * *

Apart from the occasional phone call home to mom for additional funds, I only communicated with my family when I returned from Georgetown during holiday breaks. My stay in the capital city was supported by a network of family members: my aunts Olive, Frances and Adina, and my uncle Samuel and his wife aunt Nan. They all welcomed me into their homes for extended periods while I attended High School. Not only did I survive, but I matured and became a more focused young man determined to succeed at both football and academics. I am thus eternally grateful to the helpful hands of my above-mentioned relatives. Surely, they made my road to success less burdensome with their kindness.

* * *

The school bus turned into my street in Tucber and veered slowly off the narrow concrete road onto the wider, grassy sidewalk in front of my home. It was approximately 4:30 pm in the afternoon and mom was home from work. I held my breath as she opened the door. She greeted me and my classmates cheerfully as I peered anxiously over her shoulder looking for any sign of dad. Mom read my mind.

"Your father isn't home Gregory," she said. I breathed a sigh of relief and proceeded to entertain my teachers and fellow students with snacks of fruits from my backyard. Mom, the consummate conversationalist, engaged us with stories I had heard a thousand times. Each new version was slightly different, but equally entertaining.

"It's time to go," the bus driver announced. We boarded the bus and took off to catch the 5:30 pm ferry at the New Amsterdam harbor. As we departed, an older, disheveled gentleman with silver hair waved frantically to us from the street. He scanned the faces framed through the open windows of the bus with a wide, toothless smile. He was looking for a familiar face. My dad had actually seen the bus pull away from our driveway as he returned home

from one of his adventures. He hurried to catch up to us before we left but, much to my relief, he didn't make it.

"Who is that old man?" a student asked. I didn't answer. I slowly raised my head and looked over my shoulder through the rear window of the bus.

The old man, my poor dad, stood in the distance, in the middle of the road…..still waving. He was only forty nine years old.

Reflections

I had numerous embarrassing moments courtesy of dad's addiction. I coped by suppressing my emotions and avoiding him as much as possible. In fact, I sometimes asked mom why she didn't leave him. Clearly, he didn't want to or couldn't control his love affair with the bottle. But divorce was not an option she even pondered. She bore her cross and kept her marital vows even as her children suffered in silence.

Conditions soon changed for the worse both in the country and our home. The future seemed quite bleak. Dad, meanwhile, was growing very weak. His eyes bore the look of sad resignation.

THE FINAL YEAR

1982

Dad and I sit in the living room on the first floor of our home in Tucber Park. It is 10:00 am and mom's at work. Fiona is upstairs, pregnant. She had dropped that bombshell on mom a few weeks earlier. It was impossible to discern whether mom was upset. I didn't see any hint of anger or hear any words of derision from her. That was just another test. She prayed. She smiled. She went on with life. Suddenly, dad coughs. He clutches his chest then coughs again. I see a trace of blood trickle down the corner of his lips.

⁂

In the late 1970's, the economic conditions in Guyana shifted for the worse. The largely sugar and bauxite-based economy suffered as the demand and price of those exports plummeted on the world market. A plethora of other factors, corruption and incompetence among them, accelerated the decline in wealth and prosperity. By 1982, everyone, with the notable exception of the affluent upper class and the politically connected, felt the pinch of poverty in their pockets and on their way of life. Shortages of essential commodities such as wheat flour and cooking oil were compounded by a breakdown of basic services, such as public utilities and transportation services.

As conditions deteriorated and people became strapped for cash, a thriving, underground economy evolved. Entrepreneurs and opportunists openly engaged in various commercial business activities to supplement their income. Many became full-time traders; buying and hawking food and other necessities on the open black-market. After graduating from Saint Roses High School, I flirted with a traditional clerical job in Georgetown for several months before quitting to join the growing ranks of young, black-marketers who plied their trade on the streets of Georgetown and New Amsterdam.

* * *

In 1980, I was finally offered a government academic scholarship by the Guyana Public Service Ministry (PSM) to pursue studies at Tuskegee University in Alabama, U.S.A. This was a significant milestone for me. My dream of becoming a veterinary doctor would finally be realized. However, as was customary for all recipients of this honor, I had to first complete a one-year stint of para-military service with Guyana's National Service (GNS). I received a letter from PSM advising me of my assignment to the Papaya base of GNS.

Papaya was located deep in the tropical rainforest of Essequibo, the largest of Guyana's three counties[16] It was a fifteen hour trip from Georgetown; the first twelve, a boat ride on rough seas, the final three a hike by foot on a dusty, seemingly endless trail over soaring hills with peaks that appeared to touch the sky. As we moved through the cavernous valleys, we were guided by a smiling, Amerindian fellow, who kept saying, *"We almost there boss...we almost there."* All I saw in the sweltering 100-degree

---

[16] Berbice and Demerara are the other two counties

heat were mirages in the distance on an empty, winding trail bordered by giant trees, with no end in sight. We probably had another fifteen miles to go; a stroll in the park for our enthusiastic guide.

Sergeant Major "Chip Chip" was his moniker. He was a senior officer in GNS who was assigned to the Papaya center. We met serendipitously on the boat ride from Georgetown.

"What's your name, hon?" I asked, flirting with a sapodilla-brown sweetie seated next to me on the ferry.

"Serena. What's yours?" she offered, with a smile. My response was interrupted by the gruff voice of a lanky, older man with graying hair who was leaning casually over the boat's railing. He flicked the butt of his cigarette angrily into the sea and approached us.

"Serena. Didn't I tell you not to speak to any of these no-good boys on this boat?"

It was the voice of Sergeant Major "Chip Chip". He glared at me. I shook my head and, with a derisive laugh, turned away. This incident started a feud that would make my student life at the base most discomfiting. A full day after leaving Georgetown by boat, we arrived, exhausted and starving, at the GNS Papaya Center.

A huge metal double gate opened to several acres of perfectly aligned wooden buildings. The flag of Guyana with its colorful red, white and yellow triangles framed by a rich green border, flew at full mast above the guard hut located just inside the gates. A sea of lean athletic bodies all clad in green khaki uniforms flooded the paved roads and open spaces between the buildings. Some marched, some jogged, others walked; all seemingly engaged in some purposeful activity like an organized colony of human soldier ants.

I was assigned to a unit comprised of a combination of students from the University of Guyana and the Public Service Ministry who were recently awarded scholarships to pursue their college-education overseas. I belonged to the latter.

National Service was designed to teach young Guyanese men and women self-discipline, a strong work ethic, patriotism, leadership, and military and vocational skills that would make them proud and productive citizens. It was primarily a voluntary service but for my unit, it was mandatory. We were required to serve successfully for one full year before resuming or commencing our studies. Failure to complete this stint meant immediate revocation of the scholarship award. At least, that was the axe Sergeant Major Chip Chip and other officers in charge, held over our heads to keep us in check.

It was a rough transition for most of the members of my squad. We were a mixture of twelve male and ten female students. Most were from the city. A few of us were tough country boys un-fazed by the threats of ego-maniacs such as Sergeant Major Chip Chip. The same could not be said for the city folk, especially the ladies.

"I am not drinking anything with dead flies in it," screamed Vanessa during our first breakfast in the cafeteria at the Papaya Center. She was a shapely, well-groomed, nineteen year old beauty

from Meadowbrook Gardens, a middle to upper class community in Georgetown. She was visibly agitated by the unpleasant sight of a battalion of lifeless black flies floating on the surface of the cavernous pot of green tea. The seasoned folks, who had been on the base for a few weeks or more, simply moved the dead flies aside, ladled a fly-free portion of hot tea, poured it into their mugs, and drank. By week two, a broken and thirsty Vanessa began drinking her tea from the huge pot, dead flies and all.

A typical day at Papaya started at 4:30 am with Sergeant Everton Paul (dad's nephew as fate would have it) barging into our dorm, snapping on all the lights yelling, *"Wake up ladies!"* as he struck the frames of our metal bunk beds until everyone woke up, dressed and lined up outside for the ten mile morning run.

After the mini-marathon, we ate our usual breakfast with dead flies, then returned to our dorms to shower and dress in our parrot-green uniforms, canvas caps and yachting boots (sneakers). We cleaned our dorms and meticulously prepared our beds for inspection by Sergeant Paul. If the sheets were wrinkle-free, the blankets precisely folded and our personal effects neatly stacked on the shelves, we passed inspection and proceeded to our morning assignment of clearing land, building a new dorm or painting fences. This was followed by two-hours of military drills on the dusty parade grounds in blinding sun and simmering heat. A few students collapsed on the very first day of drills from heat-stroke. Everyone felt dizzy. Sergeant Major "Chip Chip" warned that only the unconscious would be given attention and they had to first fall forward on their faces. Falling any other way would be considered a deliberate attempt to deceive the drill sergeant and the perpetrator would experience, up close and personal, traumatic retribution from the sadistic mind of the Sergeant Major. It was going to be a long year.

During my third week at Papaya, I was assigned with a group of students to clear brush in a wooded area. One foggy morning, we were all wielding our machetes vigorously against the stubborn roots of wild bushes when Sergeant Major "Chip Chip" walked by. Someone yelled, *"Chip Chip, you're an old fool."*

"Who said that?" The Sergeant Major was livid as he scanned the snickering faces in my unit. His eyes lit up when he saw me. *"You! Gregory! Yes, you with the big head. You disrespectful piece of shit! Come here!"* The snickering turned to laughter as I rose reluctantly and sauntered over. *"Shut up all of you,"* bellowed the irate officer. *"Sergeant Paul, escort this insubordinate idiot to the jailhouse immediately. I shall teach him a lesson he'll never forget."*

I spent nine hours in 'jail' reading girlie magazines and chatting with the guards. They released me just in time for dinner. I resolved to find a way to get even with the Sergeant Major.

His 'girl' Serena and I shared guard duty on the center and we soon became friends. One evening while on duty, she told me that her relationship with the Sergeant Major was merely one of convenience. I must confess that by no measure was I ever in the league of the smooth operators at Papaya, but I seized this opportunity to get to know her on a more intimate level. I had to be extremely cautious, however, as it was not uncommon for the Sergeant Major to make a surprise appearance to check up on his 'sweetie'. But Serena, a full twenty years younger than her sugar daddy, yearned for a younger lover - a virile, horny, hot-blooded nineteen year old stud.

I obliged and we consummated our lust hastily in the bushes of Papaya using our uniforms as blankets. The fear of being caught or bitten by some reptile intensified the passion of our erotic escapade. My heart skipped a few beats as she bared her full, supple breasts. Animal instincts took charge as our lips met and our naked bodies locked in a rhythmic sensual dance of pure ecstasy. I was in heaven and Serena was my angel, at least for those precious passionate moments.

.A few weeks later, I was transferred to the Kimbia National Service Center on the banks of the Berbice River to complete the final phase of national service. I never saw Serena or Sergeant Major "Chip Chip" again.

A bit of bad news awaited me when I returned home after having successfully finished my National Service stint. I opened a letter from the Public Service Ministry advising me that, due to unforeseen economic constraints, all current and future academic scholarship awards were being canceled. I was devastated.

I had applied to several universities in the United States and, like my late brother Donald, was accepted by Tuskegee University in Alabama pending the submission of my S.A.T scores and evidence of financial support. I scored well on the exam but the unfortunate news from P.S.M. meant that my dreams of becoming a veterinary doctor had to be placed on hold, indefinitely.

I contemplated my future. There weren't many attractive options; the University of Guyana did not offer a veterinary medical program and though I briefly considered joining the army as a cadet officer, I later decided that wasn't such a good idea. So, like Liz, I became a trader.

For several years, starting in the late 1970's Liz traveled extensively to neighboring Surinam and Brazil to purchase inventory. Fiona and I often assisted her in the boutique while she was away on her business trips. The money rolled in abundantly. Liz saved her profits and when the time was right, immigrated to North America, leaving the boutique in the hands of mom and a few of her close friends. For reasons unknown, the business soured in Liz's absence. Running a business was probably not one of mom's strengths so, after receiving the bad news from PSM, I ventured into the retail business and ran Liz's boutique full-time.

* * *

My poor dad and I started having frequent conversations about his glory days. I supposed he felt I was old enough to engage in manly talk. He proudly recalled his prowess, back in the day, as a ladies man. In one memorable tale, he and mom attended a wedding together and my dad, the Casanova, left the reception with another woman for a quickie, returning later to take his wife home. I had mixed feelings about his escapades. After all, he was cheating on my mother and bragging to her son about it. But adultery and fornication were both very common in the Guyanese culture. Men, like my dad, who cheated on their wives openly were revered among their peers, while female cheaters were labeled as worthless whores.

It was in this depraved environment that many young men felt compelled to engage in sexual promiscuity both in and out of wedlock. Not surprisingly, every member of my immediate family – mom, dad, Liz, Fiona and I – participated in pre-marital sexual activity.

* * *

"Make…some…..sugar….water….for…me… son," dad pleaded desperately, coughing and clutching his mouth to prevent the blood from pouring out. This solution was his home-made remedy for his liver problems. But the sugar-water didn't help. His liver was shot. He coughed uncontrollably as blood seeped between his fingers, running down the back of his right hand on to his bare chest. I called the ambulance. The medics took him to New Amsterdam Hospital. He died the next day. The cause of death: cirrhosis of the liver secondary to chronic alcohol abuse.

Reflections

And thus ended the diary of an alcohol addict's son; seventeen years of anguish, joy and pain, starting from my earliest memory as a four or five year-old to my dad's death in 1982.

Having experienced alcohol addiction first hand, I am convinced that there is really no hope for the truly dependent alcoholic without dramatic intervention. It's practically impossible for an addict to become clean on his (her) own. It's a disease that reprograms the mind. All of the learned values and principles of decency, décor and religion are ignored, thrown out the window, by the alcohol addict. Nothing in life is more important than that next drink.

How sad.

How true.

ELEGY

FIFTY TWO GOING ON SEVENTY

Destiny dealt a crushing blow

that fateful day in June

as we sat in our modest living room

reliving his glory days / of fierce firefights braved

and numerous lives saved / of recognitions and commendations /

of his meteoric rise to the highest rank at his station…

I perused his wrinkled smiling face / framed by a thick bristling

crown of gray / and wondered what might have been

had he not succumbed to the lure of Addiction

that hijacked his ambition / as she flew from casual flirtation

to hopeless dependency / as his tolerance waned from several

hours at the village bar / to a few sips and ultimately,

to a stage where a mere whiff led to inebriation…

I locked my despair and discomfiture in a closet

filled with mixed juvenile emotions / as I witnessed up close and

personal / this decadence / this destruction / this depravation …

Red rivulets rush from the corners of his parched lips,

slip between his quivering fingers and

drip…drip…drip…

to the tiled floor

as he coughs uncontrollably / and beckons to me desperately

to hurry/ to help / to heal…

But decades of abuse had taken its toll

and his cirrhotic liver would function no more…

He departed the next day…

Fifty-two going on seventy…

EPILOGUE

My poor dad started drinking in his teens under duress, continued drinking voluntarily, became addicted, mentally ill, lost his job, did time in jail, embarrassed everyone around him, traumatized his family, neglected his children, and died a tragic caricature of his former self, at the age of fifty two. At the time of his death, he looked more like seventy one. Alcohol seduced him. Alcohol abused him. Alcohol destroyed him. It consumed his mind, crushed his spirit, corroded his liver, and caused every bit of promise he possessed to remain unfulfilled.

Alcohol addiction stole my father from me.

In case you are wondering whether my dad's alcohol problem had any significant lasting effects on my adult life. Let me assure you that it did to some degree. For example, I only drink casually and I am always conscious of the fact that there is a genetic connection to alcoholism; that I may have a predisposition passed down from my father to also become addicted to alcohol. So I drink with extreme caution. In other words, I am a paranoid drinker.

From an academic and professional standpoint, I have done reasonably well. I earned a Bachelor of Science degree in biosciences from Tuskegee University in Alabama and an MBA in marketing from Saint John's University in New York. I am presently working on a doctorate in international business and economics at Pace University. On occasion, I imagine that my dad is living vicariously through me. I often wonder what might have been, how my life would have been different, had dad not been an alcoholic? I guess I'll never know.

But anyway, I am happily married to June, whom I met in Brooklyn, New York in 1991 and we have three boys: Sean, James Jr., and Jalani. We live in a cozy home in the suburbs of Atlanta, Georgia; and from all appearances, we are a happy and well-adjusted family.

As for my sisters; Fiona has two master's degrees and is an independent Special Education Consultant and successful

entrepreneur. She is married to Troy and has three children –
Randy, Anthony and Tricia. Liz has an associate degree in
computer technology. She is divorced and has two daughters,
Gwendolyn and Wislyne, and two grandchildren. She is a realtor.
My other sister, Sybil, is a nurse and is also happily married to
Michael. She has three children. My half-brothers, dad's sons,
Donald and Brian, as previously mentioned were both tragically
killed; the former in a drowning accident at Kimbia, the latter at
the hands of a crazed criminal who bludgeoned him to death in
Georgetown.

Mom is retired and residing in her home in Tucber Park, New
Amsterdam, Guyana.

So we haven't done too badly. Looking back, things could have
easily been a lot worse. But are there lessons to be learned and
shared from dad's tragic addiction to alcohol?

Was his life a total waste?

Or does it have some redeeming value?

The answers are yes, no and yes, respectively. And these answers underscore the primary focus of "My Poor Dad".

LITERATURE REVIEW AND DISCUSSION

In the introduction, I reflected on why society has failed to effectively solve the problem of alcohol addiction. Let's take a closer look at this issue.

In order to solve a problem, any problem, it is necessary to have a clear understanding of what the problem is, to identify direct and indirect causative variables, and to develop and implement realistic and practical solutions that incorporate these variables. Sounds relatively simple, right?

Unfortunately, in the case of alcohol addiction, it is not.

My review of empirical data on the etiology and treatment of alcohol abuse was quite revealing. I discovered that while there are two major paradigms used to study alcohol abuse (the objectivist and subjectivist approaches[17]), there is a plethora of variables

---

[17] Peyrot, Mark. THE ETIOLOGY AND TREATMENT OF SUBSTANCE ABUSE. The International Journal of Sociology and Social Policy; 1996; Vol. 16; Issues 5/6; pgs 178 – 195

directly and indirectly related to the problem of alcohol addiction. In other words, it is extremely complex. This complexity is further exacerbated by the fact that alcohol is legal, abundantly available and marketed aggressively to everyone, especially the young demographic in their twenties and thirties. In reality, many alcoholics confess to having had their first drink in their pre-teen years.

Let's examine the two approaches a little more closely. In the objectivist paradigm, alcohol abuse is taken for granted and the emphasis is placed on causative factors (see research by Hood, Liu and Kaplan). The subjectivist paradigm (also known as "constructionist") digs deeper. The lens is focused on the nature of the abuse itself. There are three sub-divisions to this approach: "vulgar", "strict" and "contextual" constructionism (Best, 1995).

The first one -"vulgar" - compares the problem's social definition to its objective state.

The second approach – "strict" – only examines the subject process (or construction).

The third, "contextual" constructionism explores factors related to the successful implementation of definitions.

To further complicate matters, empirical researchers have identified a host of factors related to the initiation and escalation of alcohol use and abuse.

Buwick, Martin and Martin (1988) discovered a vicious cycle of dysfunction between children and alcohol-abusing parents often resulting in the children becoming substance abusers themselves. Consequently, Schmidt (1994) stated that these alarming results mandated "a critical need for education and counseling services for students..." However, he observed that a destructive paradox existed in the school systems in that counselors, schools and social service agencies are often unclear of their roles resulting in counter-productive turf wars instead of constructive cooperation to help at-risk students and families.

Liu and Kaplan observed significant differences between males and females, with the former drinking to attain "a sense of disinhibition and power" and the latter "drinking to self-medicate psychosocial distress…". .

Hood's research found a positive correlation between earlier onset of alcohol use and the escalation of problematic behaviors.

Similarly, Brownlee and Anderson (1988) identified a "rapid escalation in the initiation of alcohol and drug abuse among youths through the middle school years".

Booth and Feng (2002) studied the effects of alcohol consumption and the related consequences on short-term employment. They discovered that employed people who drank seven or more drinks per day were significantly less likely to go to work; and the likelihood of continued unemployment increased significantly for unemployed drinkers with similar frequencies of alcohol consumption.

So what ?

What does all of this mean to the alcoholic, to me, to you, to the family and friends of alcoholics, to their employers, to society in general?

These empirical findings emphasize the need for:

1) Better leadership, commitment and cooperation among public officials, schools and parents, to proactively and effectively address and resolve the problem of the use and abuse of alcohol by children;

2) Unique treatment approaches to address the differences among abusers of alcohol such as gender, education, race, ethnicity, income and marital status;

3) Early intervention to prevent the transition from casual to habitual and addictive alcohol consumption;

4) Greater investment of public and private financial and professional resources to support interventional measures to reduce drinking among at-risk drinkers.

Remember that there is no quick fix for a problem as complex as addiction. It literally takes a village to increase awareness, to identify those at risk, to intervene, to sustain, to support, and to fight the hard battles necessary to simply put a dent in this destructive colossus.

RESOURCES TO FIGHT ALCOHOL ADDICTION

What can you do to make a difference to your child, brother, sister, friend, colleague, mom or even dad who may be at risk, or who may already be an addict? The answer is - a whole lot. A whole lot more than I or my mom or sisters ever could.

The internet is a tremendous resource for information on any alcohol-related subject matter. There are a number of addiction-support centers and hotlines in every state of America. I have found the following websites to be particularly useful:

1. http://alcoholism.about.com/od/about/Alcoholism_101.htm

The format is very user-friendly. The categories and links include

a) Topics such as Alcohol 101 which provides the basics of alcoholism, How to Quit, Find an Alcohol Anonymous meeting near you, College drinking, etc.

b) Articles and Resources which links to information on topics such as Alcohol Abuse vs. Alcohol Dependence, Hitting Bottom, Genetics and Alcoholism, How to Quit, Problem Drinkers, and What Do We Mean by Alcoholism.

2. http://www.healthline.com

3. http://www.info.org

4. http://www.Alcohol.Rehabilitation.Org

5. http://www.MayoClinic.com

6. http://www.rehabilitationdrug.biz – the top alcohol rehabilitation programs in the US are listed here (see the short list below).

7. http://www.gatewaytorecovery.com - another source for detox-rehab-outpatient programs.

Here is a short list of alcohol rehabilitation programs in the US (source - http://www.rehabilitationdrug.biz) :

1. Online Drug and Alcohol Treatment Guide/Directory – http://www.drugalcoholcenters.com - an exhaustive list of in-patient and out-patient rehab services and centers.

2. 1-866-SOBERNOW.COM   –   http://www.1-866-sobernow.com – 24/7 drug referral service that will help you find the right drug rehab program to fit your needs.

3. Our Master's Camp – http://www.ourmasterscamp.org – TELEPHONE: 1-423-447-2340; Christian-based drug rehab program located on 90 acres in Pikeville, Tennessee.

4. Laurel   Canyon   Recovery   Center   – http://laurelcanyoncenter.com – TELEPHONE: 1-888-300-5080; located in historic Hollywood Hills, California and designed to look like the exclusive Newport Beach. A rehab facility for creative people such as artists, writers, musicians, actors, and entrepreneurs.

5. Holistic   Addiction   Treatment   Center   – http://www.drugrehabcenter.com – 24/7 HOTLINE: 1-866-358-0308; email: help@drugrehabcenter.com

6. A   Better   Tomorrow   –   http://www.abttc.com   –   24/7

HOTLINE: 1-800-971-1586

And this is just the tip of the iceberg. A wealth of information is

available to help the addicted. I wish my family had access to one

of these services. But it's too late for us. Alcohol destroyed my

dad's life. Don't let it destroy yours or that of someone you know

and love.

Take action today!

Reach out and help...please!

---

[1] Merriam-Webster's COLLEGIATE DICTIONARY – Tenth Edition
[2] Booth, Brenda M., Feng W. THE IMPACT OF DRINKING AND DRINKING CONSEQUENCES IN
SHORT-TERM EMPLOYMENT OUTCOMES IN AT-RISK DRINKERS IN SIX SOUTHERN STATES.
The Journal of Behavioral Health Services & Research. Gaithersburg: May 2002. Vol.29, Iss. 2; pg. 157-
167.

Biography

Pablo (James G.D. Paul)

Born and raised in Guyana, an English-speaking West Indian nation located on the northern coast of South America, Pablo earned a national academic scholarship to pursue his college education overseas.

Inspired by a poem from his sister-in-law, Paula Stewart, he embraced his gift of writing, publishing four books of poetry and his first novel, My Poor Dad, between February 2007 and January 2008.

Pablo is a pharmaceutical sales and marketing consultant by profession.

For more information please email jpaul591@hotmail.com or visit Pablo's websites: www.blogetrylyrics.com , www.myspace.com/jp591 and www.poeTeez.com

www.ingramcontent.com/pod-product-compliance
Lightning Source LLC
Chambersburg PA
CBHW050309260626
47156CB00005B/1728